The Museum Mice in Winter

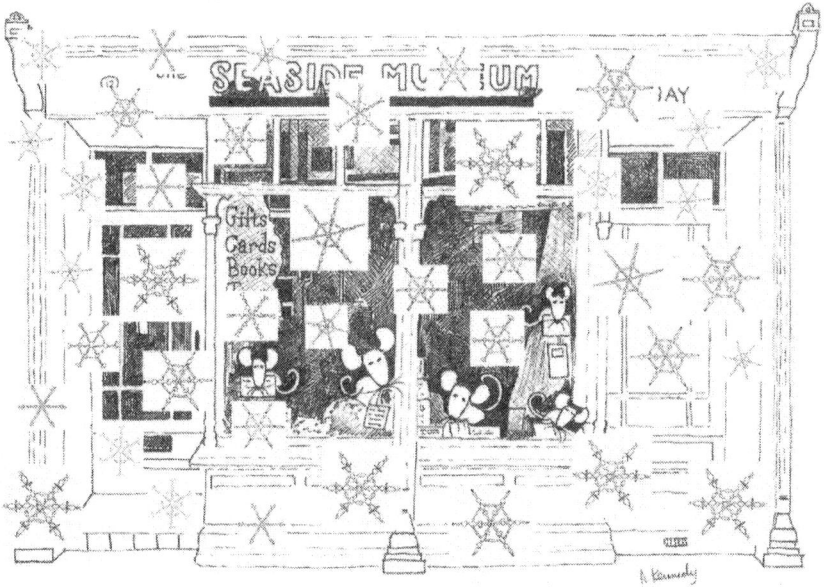

Winter Stories

By Mrs Mandy Mouse

and Dianne Long

Illustrations by Angela Kennedy

Published in association with the Seaside
Museum, Herne Bay, 12 William Street, Herne Bay,
Kent

@seasidemuseum

www.theseasidemuseum.org

Table of Contents

Other Books About the Museum Mice

The Museum Mice of Herne Bay

Contains three summer stories about the

museum mice

A Winter Day in Herne Bay

It was a very cold day. Anna and Tom were going to the Seaside Museum to find out about Storytime. Then they were going out for lunch.

The Big People arrived at the Museum. Anna and Tom saw the Museum Mice.

'Do you want to

come out for lunch?' Anna said.

'Yes please,' said Mr and Mrs Mouse.

'Yes please,' said Monty Mouse.

'Yes please,' said Maisie Mouse.

'Yes please,' said Max Mouse.

Monty, Maisie and Max got into Anna's pocket.

Mr and Mrs Mouse got into Tom's pocket.

They went into the café. Anna and Tom put the mice on a statue outside the café.

'Wait here', said Anna. 'We will ask Joe and Shane to bring some food out for you.'

The mice settled down to wait.

'What is this statue?' asked Monty.

'It is very interesting,' said Maisie.

'It is very big,' said Max.

'It is a bird,' said Mrs Mouse.

'It is a heron,' said Mr Mouse.

'The heron is the symbol of the town of Herne Bay,' said Mrs Mouse.

Anna and Tom were a long time. They were inside the café having lunch. The mice could not go in the café. Mice were not allowed.

Just then the door of the café opened. Joe and Shane came out carrying a small bowl of hot soup.

They put it down near the Museum
Mice with some bread.

Joe and Shane waved and the
Museum Mice waved back.

'Thank you,' squeaked Mr and
Mrs Mouse.

'Thank you,' squeaked the little mice.

The Museum Mice started to eat. They dipped the bread into the hot soup.

'Lovely,' said Mr Mouse.

'Delicious,' said Mrs Mouse.

'Tasty,' said Monty, Maisie and Max. 'Very, very tasty.'

Soon it was all finished. Joe and Shane came to collect the bowl. The

Museum Mice thanked them again.

'Brr,' said Mr Mouse. 'It is getting colder.'

'I am cold,' said Monty.

'Put your hat on,' said Mrs Mouse.

Monty's hat was old. It was not

very warm. But he put it on.

'I am cold,' said Maisie.

'Put your scarf on,' said Mrs Mouse.

Maisie's scarf was old. It was not very warm. But she put it on.

'I am cold too,' said Max.

'Put your gloves on,' said Mrs Mouse.

Max's gloves were old. They were not very warm. But he put

them on.

'Look at the sky,' said Mrs Mouse.

They all looked at the sky. It was very grey.

Snowflakes started to fall.

'It is snowing,' said Monty.

'It is snowing hard,' said Maisie.

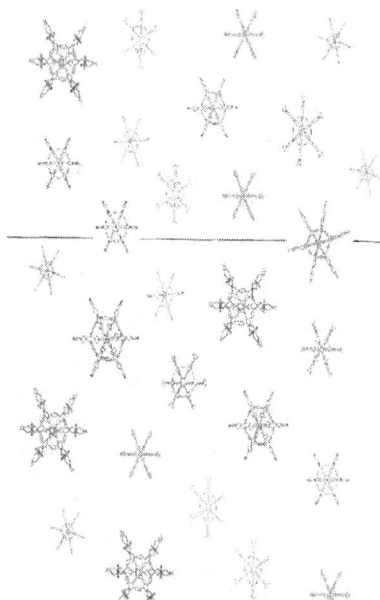

'It is snowing fast,' said Max.

'Snow, snow, snow, wonderful snow,' shouted Monty.

'Snow, snow, snow, marvellous snow,' shouted Maisie.

'Snow, snow, snow, fabulous snow,' shouted Max excitedly.

'Hooray!' said Monty.

'Hooray!' said Maisie.

'Hooray!' said Max.

'It is very cold,' said Mr Mouse.

The Big People came out of the café. Tom put the Museum Mice in his pocket and took them back to the Seaside Museum.

In the Museum, Mrs Long was talking to some children.

She was showing them some old photographs of Herne Bay in the snow.

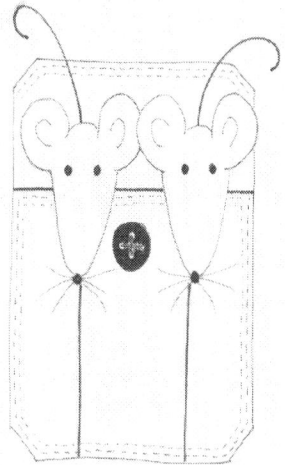

'In 1963 the snow lasted for weeks. I was a little girl at the time and I can remember it,' said Mrs Long. 'It was a long time ago.'

After the children had gone home, Mrs Long left the photos on the table. Then she went home.

The mice went to have a look at the old photographs. The photographs showed deep snow on the seafront and in the park.

'It looks very cold in the photographs,' said Monty.

'It looks very icy in the photographs,' said Maisie.

'It looks very snowy in the photographs,' said Max.

'Look at this,' said Mr Mouse.

He showed them photographs of

the pier and the sea.

'It looks very, very cold,' said Monty.

'What is wrong with the sea in this picture?' asked Maisie.

'It looks all white and rough,' said Max.

'The sea froze because it was so very cold,' said Mr Mouse.

'The sea froze a long way out,' said Mrs Mouse.

'Yes,' said Mr Mouse. 'It has happened several times in the last one hundred years.'

'Will the sea freeze tomorrow?' asked Monty.

'I hope it does,' said Maisie.

'I would like to see that,' said Max.

The mice were getting hungry again.

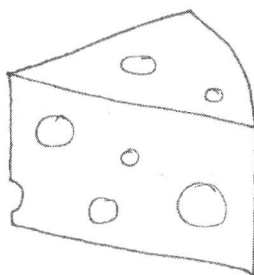

'It is time for supper,' said Mr Mouse.

He found some cheese and some apples left behind by the Big People who worked in the museum shop.

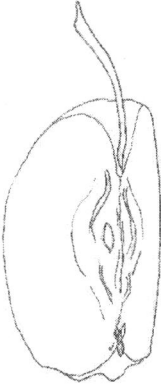

Mrs Mouse shared the food out.

Mr Mouse had some cheese.

Mrs Mouse had a bit of apple.

Monty Mouse had some cheese.

Maisie Mouse had some apple.

Max Mouse had some apple.

They all enjoyed their supper.

After supper, it was still snowing. They went over to the window. They looked out. It was snowing hard.

Big, white, fluffy snowflakes were coming down. The pavement outside the museum was covered with thick, white, soft snow.

'It looks very beautiful,' said Mrs Mouse.

'It is getting very deep,' said Monty.

'It looks like a blanket,' said Maisie.

'A soft, fluffy blanket,' said Max.

Talking about blankets made the little mice feel tired.

'Time for bed now,' said Mrs

Mouse.

The little mice washed their paws and faces before going to bed.

'Do not forget to clean your teeth and tails,' called Mr Mouse.

At last they were ready for bed.

Monty Mouse went to sleep in a long pointed shell.

Maisie Mouse went to sleep in a curly round shell.

Max Mouse went to sleep in a small brown shell.

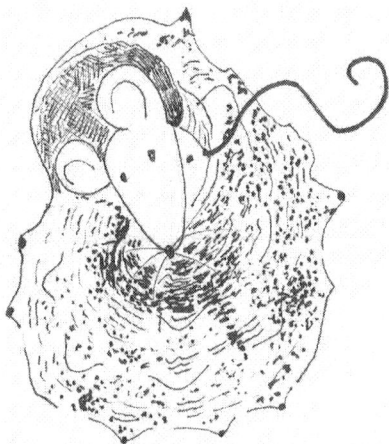

Mr and Mrs Mouse went to sleep in an oyster shell.

They pulled the covers up to their ears to keep warm.

Monty Mouse called out, 'Will we be able to build a snow mouse tomorrow?'

Maisie Mouse called out, 'I want to build a snow mouse.'

Max Mouse said quietly, 'A snow mouse, a snow mouse,' just as his eyes closed.

'Yes,' said Mr Mouse.

All the mice went to sleep in their seashell beds.

They dreamt of building a snow
mouse in the deep white snow.

All through the night the
snowflakes fell from the sky to
cover the path outside the Seaside

Museum.

''A snow mouse, a snow mouse,'
mumbled Max in his dreamy sleep.

When he woke up the next
morning he scampered over to the
window. It was still snowing.

He washed and dressed and went
downstairs.

He ate his breakfast – cheese of
course! – and then he put on his
outdoor clothes.

He went outside.

Monty and Maisie joined him.

Together they built a snow
mouse!

The Museum Mice at Christmas

Once upon a time, the museum mice were waiting for the museum to close so they could go foraging for food.

'Have the Big People gone home yet?' asked Monty Mouse.

'No,' said Mrs Mouse. 'I can still hear them talking.'

'What are they saying?' asked Maisie Mouse.

'They are saying they will never be finished in time for Christmas,' said Mrs Mouse.

'What does that mean?' asked Max Mouse.

'I do not know,' said Mrs Mouse.

'Sh, or they will hear us,' said Mr Mouse.

The little mice were quiet, as quiet as mice.

They heard the door opening and then closing again. The Big People had gone home.

The mice scampered downstairs.

'I want to find an apple,' said Monty Mouse.

'I want to find some cheese,'

said Maisie Mouse.

'I want to find some cheese too,' said Max Mouse.

'We must all look for cheese,' said Mrs Mouse.

'Let us see who can be first to find some,' said Mr Mouse.

The Big People brought sandwiches to work.

Sometimes they left crumbs of bread and cheese behind.

Sometimes they left crumbs of bread and jam behind.

And sometimes they left other things behind as well.

Monty Mouse found a sparkly blue bauble on the shelf.

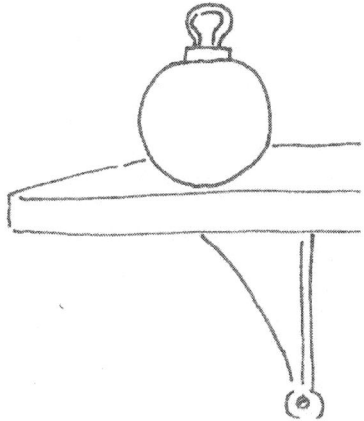

Maisie Mouse found a sparkly yellow bauble under the counter.

Max Mouse found a sparkly red bauble behind the chair.

Mrs Mouse found a sparkly silver bauble over the banister.

And Mr Mouse found a green tree by the door!

'What is a tree doing inside?' asked Monty Mouse.

'It is a Christmas tree!' said Mrs Mouse.

'People like to decorate trees at

Christmas,' said Mr Mouse. 'They bring them inside and cover them with sparkly baubles.'

'The Big People did not have time to finish decorating the tree before they went home. Let us help them,' said Mrs Mouse.

So Monty Mouse hung the sparkly blue

bauble on the tree.

Maisie Mouse hung the sparkly yellow bauble on the tree.

Max Mouse hung the sparkly red bauble on the tree.

Mrs Mouse hung the sparkly silver bauble on the tree.

Mr Mouse said, 'The tree looks very nice. But I think it needs something to go on the top.'

He looked around and he found a

gold star.

'This will go on the top of the tree,' he said.

They all looked at the top of the

tree. It was a long way up.

It was too high for Monty to reach.

It was too high for Maisie to reach.

It was too high for Max to reach.

It was too high for Mrs Mouse to reach.

It was even too high for Mr Mouse to reach.

'What shall we do?' asked Mr

Mouse.

'I know,' said Mrs Mouse to Mr Mouse. 'If I stand on your shoulders, and Monty stands on my shoulders, and Maisie stands on Monty's shoulders and Max stands on Maisie's shoulders, we might be able to reach the top.'

So Mrs Mouse stood on Mr Mouse's shoulders.

Monty stood on Mrs Mouse's

shoulders.

Maisie stood on Monty Mouse's shoulders.

And Max stood on Maisie's shoulders.

But they still could not reach the top.

'Come down, children. Max, you come first,' said Mr Mouse.

But Max was starting to wobble.

He wobbled a bit at first. Then

he wobbled a lot.

It made Maisie wobble.

It made Monty wobble.

It made Mrs Mouse wobble.

Then it made Mr Mouse wobble and they all came tumbling down.

'Oh dear,' said Mr Mouse.

Luckily, no one was hurt.

'That was not a good idea,' said Mr Mouse. 'The star is too big for us to carry it all the way up the tree.'

Monty Mouse was looking round the museum.

'Look what I have found,' he said.

'It is a piece of gold string,' said Maisie Mouse.

'It is all shiny,' said Max Mouse.

'It is not string, it is tinsel,' said Mr Mouse. 'The Big People use it to decorate their homes at Christmas.'

'I have an idea,' said Monty

Mouse.

He tied the tinsel to the star and then he scampered up the tree, holding on to the tinsel in his teeth. He dragged the star up behind him.

'Well done, Monty,' said Mrs Mouse.

'Where did you find the tinsel?' Maisie Mouse asked.

'In a box under the counter,' said Monty Mouse.

The box had lots of shiny decorations spilling out of it.

'Oh, pretty!' said Maisie, clapping her front paws.

'Shiny!' shouted Max, then fell over in his excitement.

Maisie held Max's paw and they went over to the box.

There was a lot of tinsel inside. They took it out and scampered up the tree, trailing the tinsel behind them.

When they were high enough

they let go of the tinsel and it settled around the tree.

'There is another box,' said Monty Mouse. 'This one is behind the counter.'

The box was full of shiny baubles.

'Let us hang them on the tree,' said Mr Mouse. 'Be careful, they are fragile.'

They hung all the baubles on the

tree. They had been so busy they had not noticed the time. It was light outside. The museum was about to open.

Mrs Mouse heard the key in the door.

'Quick, children,' she said. 'Run back upstairs.'

'But we did not find any cheese,' said Monty Mouse.

'There is no time for cheese,'

said Mrs Mouse. 'Run!'

They all ran upstairs.

They were very tired after all their work. Mrs Mouse tucked them all up in their little beds.

When they woke up the next morning the museum was very quiet. They could not wait to go downstairs!

They scampered down the stairs as fast as they could.

The Christmas tree was looking very pretty. Under the tree was a parcel wrapped in Christmas wrapping paper. It had a label on it. The label said: For the Museum

Mice. Merry Christmas. Love from Anna and Tom.

'We had better open the parcel,' said Mr Mouse.

So Mrs Mouse opened it

There was a new coat and a big
piece of cheese
for Mr Mouse.

There was a
new skirt and a
medium sized
piece of cheese
for Mrs Mouse.

There was a new hat and a small

piece of cheese for Monty Mouse.

There was a new scarf and a
small piece of cheese for Maisie

Mouse.

There was a new pair of gloves and a tiny piece of cheese for Max mouse.

They all sat down to eat.

'How lucky we are,' said Mr Mouse.

'All these lovely presents for us,' said Mrs Mouse. 'And all this lovely cheese!'

She licked her lips.

'This is the best Christmas ever,'

said Monty Mouse. 'My new hat will keep me warm. It covers my ears so they will not get cold.'

'My new scarf will keep me warm,' said Maisie Mouse. 'It is all soft and cosy.'

'My new gloves will keep me warm,' said Max Mouse. 'But the present I liked best of all was the cheese!'

A Winter Mystery

It was a cold day. The Seaside
Museum was busy.
There were lots of
Big People in the
shop. There were
children in the
museum enjoying a craft activity.

Anna and Tom were busy
making cards.

They saw the Museum Mice.

Anna said, 'We are going shopping soon. Would you like to come with us?'

'Yes please,' said Monty Mouse.

'Yes please,' said Maisie Mouse.

'Yes please,' said Max Mouse.

When Anna and Tom had finished the cards they helped the mice into their bag.

They all left the museum. The

Museum Mice peered over the top of the bag.

'Everywhere looks very busy,' said Monty.

'Yes, very busy,' said Maisie.

'Lots and lots of people,' said Max.

Anna and Tom walked along Mortimer Street.

It was Saturday so there were lots of market stalls.

'Look, there is a stall where you can buy books,' said Monty.

'This stall has bread and cakes,' said Maisie.

'You can buy toys at this stall,' said Max.

Tom bought a
toy car.

Anna bought a
book and a tiny
jigsaw in a
matchbox for the
Museum Mice.

'Thank you,'
said Monty.

'Thank you,' said Maisie.

'Thank you,' said Max.

They all watched the Big People buy bread, eggs and vegetables.

It was very exciting.

Anna and Tom walked along the street. They saw a gift shop, a café and a shoe shop.

'What is that building?' asked Monty.

It was a tall building with big doors and a path outside.

'That is a church,' said Mr

Mouse.

Maisie saw a building that did
not have things for sale in the
windows.

'This is a funny shop,' she said.

'I cannot see anything to buy in

the windows,' said Monty.

'It is a bank,' said Mrs Mouse. 'The Big People save their money in a bank.'

'The bank keeps their money safe,' said Mr Mouse.

Monty, Maisie and Max watched

the Big People doing their shopping.

'What a lot of shopping,' said
Monty.

'Lots and lots of shopping,' said
Maisie.

'Lots and lots and lots,' said
Max.

They all walked along William
Street.

Opposite the Museum there was
a bright red post box. The post box

looked funny. It was wearing a hat!

'Let us go and look at the hat,' said Anna.

The post box hat was knitted. It had some black and white penguins on the top.

'Please can we go up to look at the penguins? said Monty.

Anna lifted the Museum Mice up next to the knitted penguins.

'Hello,' said Monty to the penguins.

'Hello,' said Maisie to the penguins.

'Hello,' said Max to the penguins.

But the penguins did not reply!

'The Seaside Museum has had a knitted display in the shop window,' said Mrs Mouse.

'The knitted post box hats are called "Post Box Toppers" and they are put on most post boxes in Herne Bay'.

'Yes,' said Mr Mouse. 'The Big People knit them. Each topper is different. some have snow scenes, presents, robins…'

'And penguins,' said Monty.

'And mice,' said Maisie.

'If we keep very still the Big People will not notice us', said Mr Mouse.

The mice kept very very still. They could see all the people doing their shopping. The town was very busy. Two children came to look at

the post box topper.

'Look at the penguins,' said the boy.

'Look at the little mice,' said the girl.

The mice kept very still.

'How many mice can you see?' asked the girl.

'One, two, three, four, five,' counted the boy.

The children went away.

The Museum Mice ran around the penguins looking at them.

'We are the same size,' said Monty.

Just then a man came and talked to Anna and Tom's Big People. The man told them he wanted to take a photograph of a family looking at the Post Box Toppers. The man wanted to put the photograph in the newspaper.

Anna and Tom's Big People
agreed. They all looked at the

penguins and the mice.

'Freeze, don't move,' said Mr
Mouse.

Mrs Mouse froze.

Monty Mouse froze.

Maisie Mouse froze.

Max Mouse froze.

'Smile for the photograph, say 'cheese',' said the man with the camera.

The Big People smiled.

Anna and Tom smiled.

'Cheese', said Mr Mouse.

'Cheese,' said Mrs Mouse.

Monty Mouse said, 'Cheese'.

Maisie Mouse said, 'Cheese'.

And Max Mouse said, 'Cheese'.

The man took the

photograph.

'Thank you,' said

the photographer.

Anna and Tom put

the mice in their bag when the Big

People were saying goodbye.

Anna and Tom went into the

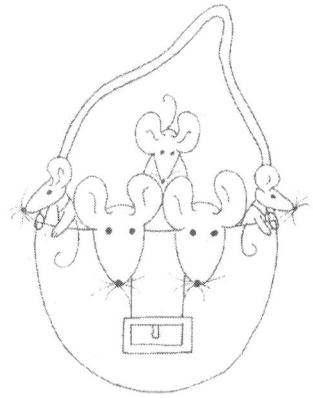

Seaside Museum to collect their
cards. The mice climbed out of the
bag. Anna gave them the jigsaw.

'Thank you,' said the mice.

They scurried away to do the
jigsaw. It was
great fun.

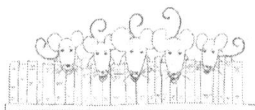

Next day,
Sandra, one of
the Big People
who worked in
the shop, was
looking at a
newspaper.

She looked at the photo of the

Post Box Topper.

The Museum Mice were sitting on a shelf watching her read.

'It is very strange,' she said.

'I have just walked by the post box and there are no mice on the top, only penguins! What a mystery. I wonder what happened to the mice.'

The Museum Mice giggled and giggled and giggled!

'We are here,' they squeaked as they scampered into hiding!

'What was that?' asked Sandra.

She looked around but she could not see them.

She folded the newspaper.

'I think it will always be a mystery!'

Printed in Great Britain
by Amazon